MR. SLOW

by Roger Hargreaves

Mr Slow, as you might well know, or maybe you don't, lived next door to Mr Busy.

He'd built his house himself.

Slowly.

It had taken him ten years!

And, as you might well know, or maybe you don't, Mr Slow talked in an extraordinarily slow way.

He . . . talked . . . like . . . this.

And every single thing he did was as slow as the way he talked.

For instance.

If Mr Slow was writing this book about himself, you wouldn't be able to read it yet.

He wouldn't even have got as far as this page!

For instance.

If Mr Slow was eating a currant cake for tea, it took him until bedtime.

He'd eat it crumb by crumb, currant by currant, chewing each crumb and each currant one hundred times.

For instance.

Last Christmas, it took Mr Slow until New Year's Day to open his Christmas presents.

And then it took him until Easter to write his thank-you letters!

Oh, he was a slow man.

Now, this story isn't about the time Mr Slow went on a picnic with Mr Busy.

That's another story.

No, this story is about the time Mr Slow decided to get a job.

He read all the job advertisements in the Sunday paper (which took him until Wednesday) and then he went and got himself a job reading the news on television.

Can you imagine?

It was very embarrassing!

"Good . . . evening . . .," said Mr Slow. "Here . . . is . . . the . . . nine . . . o' . . . clock . . . news."

It took him until midnight to read it!

And everybody who was watching went to sleep.

So, that job wasn't any good.

Was it?

Then, Mr Slow got himself a job as a taxi driver.

"Take me to the railway station," cried Mr Uppity, as he leapt into his taxi. "I have a train to catch at 3 o'clock!"

"Right . . . ho," said Mr Slow, and set off.

At one mile an hour!

And arrived at the station at 4 o'clock.

So, that job wasn't any good.

Was it?

And, that summer, Mr Slow got a job making ice cream. But, by the time he'd made the ice cream, it wasn't exactly the right sort of weather to be selling ice cream!

Brrr!

So, Mr Slow got himself a job making woolly scarves. But, by the time he'd finished making the scarves, it wasn't exactly the right sort of weather to be selling scarves!

Phew!

Poor Mr Slow.

He went around to ask the other Mr Men what he should do.

"Be a racing driver!" suggested Mr Silly.

Can you imagine?

No!

"Be an engine driver!" suggested Mr Funny.

Can you imagine?

No! No!

"Be a speedboat driver!" suggested Mr Tickle.

Can you imagine?

No! No! No!

But then, Mr Happy had an extremely good idea.

Most sensible.

"Be a steamroller driver," he suggested.

And today that is exactly what Mr Slow does.

Slowly backwards and slowly forwards he drives.

Up and down.

Down and up.

Ever so slowly.

The next time you see a steamroller doing that, look and see if Mr Slow is driving it.

If he is, you shout to him, "Hello, Mr Slow! Are you having a nice time?"

And he'll wave, and shout back to you.

"Yes . . . thank . . . you . . .," he'll shout.

"Good . . . bye!"

Fantastic offers for Mr. Men fans!

Collect all your Mr. Men or Little Miss books in these superb durable collectors' cases!

Only £5.99 inc. postage and packing, these wipe-clean, hard-wearing cases will give all your Mr. Men or Little Miss books a beautiful new home!

Keep track of your collection with this giant-sized double-sided Mr. Men and Little Miss Collectors' poster.

Collect 6 tokens and we will send you a brilliant giant-sized double-sided collectors' poster! Simply tape a £1 coin to cover postage and packaging in the space provided and fill out the form overleaf.

STICK £1 COIN HERE
(for poster only)

Only need a few Mr. Men or Little Miss to complete your set? You can order any of the titles on the back of the books from our Mr. Men order line on 0870 787 1724. Orders should be delivered between 5 and 7 working days.

— TO BE COMPLETED BY AN ADULT —

To apply for any of these great offers, ask an adult to complete the details below and send this whole page with the appropriate payment and tokens, to: MR. MEN CLASSIC OFFER, PO BOX 715, HORSHAM RH12 5WG

☐ Please send me a giant-sized double-sided collectors' poster.

AND ☐ I enclose 6 tokens and have taped a £1 coin to the other side of this page.

☐ Please send me ☐ Mr. Men Library case(s) and/or ☐ Little Miss library case(s) at £5.99 each inc P&P

☐ I enclose a cheque/postal order payable to Egmont UK Limited for £............................

OR ☐ Please debit my MasterCard / Visa / Maestro / Delta account (delete as appropriate) for £............................

Card no. ☐☐☐☐☐☐☐☐☐☐☐☐☐☐☐☐☐☐☐☐   Security code ☐☐☐

Issue no. (if available) ☐   Start Date ☐☐/☐☐/☐☐   Expiry Date ☐☐/☐☐/☐☐

Fan's name: ....   Date of birth: ....

Address: ....

....

....   Postcode: ....

Name of parent / guardian: ....

Email for parent / guardian: ....

Signature of parent / guardian: ....

Please allow 28 days for delivery. Offer is only available while stocks last. We reserve the right to change the terms of this offer at any time and we offer a 14 day money back guarantee. This does not affect your statutory rights. Offers apply to UK only.

☐ We may occasionally wish to send you information about other Egmont children's books.
If you would rather we didn't, please tick this box.

Ref: MRM 001

cut along the dotted line and return this whole page